Obama vs. McCain and the Historic Election

A MODERN PERSPECTIVES BOOK

Tamra B. Orr

Published in the United States of America by Cherry Lake Publishing
Ann Arbor, Michigan
www.cherrylakepublishing.com

Content Adviser: Satta Sarmah Hightower, Writer & Editor, Talented Tenth Media, Boston, MA
Reading Adviser: Marla Conn MS, Ed., Literacy specialist, Read-Ability, Inc.

Photo Credits: © REUTERS / Alamy Stock Photo, cover, 1; © Rawpixel.com / Shutterstock.com, 4, 5; © Baiterek Media / Shutterstock.com, 7; © Krista Kennell / Shutterstock.com, 9, 12; © mistydawnphoto / Shutterstock.com, 10;© Jack Frog / Shutterstock.com, 14; © Angela N Perryman / Shutterstock.com, 15; © EQRoy / Shutterstock.com, 17; © Jeffery Stone / Shutterstock.com, 19; © gary718 / Shutterstock.com, 20; © Uber Images / Shutterstock.com, 22; © Action Sports Photography / Shutterstock.com, 23; © Schomburg Center for Research in Black Culture, Photographs and Prints Division, The New York Public Library, 25; © Everett Collection / Shutterstock.com, 27; © Juli Hansen / Shutterstock.com, 30

Graphic Element Credits: ©RoyStudioEU/Shutterstock.com, back cover, front cover, multiple interior pages; ©queezz/Shutterstock.com, back cover, front cover, multiple interior pages

Library of Congress Cataloging-in-Publication Data has been filed and is available at catalog.loc.gov

Cherry Lake Publishing would like to acknowledge the work of The Partnership for 21st Century Skills. Please visit *www.p21.org* for more information.

Printed in the United States of America
Corporate Graphics

Table of Contents

In this book, you will read three different perspectives about the 2008 presidential election between Barack Obama and John McCain, which happened on November 4, 2008. While these characters are fictionalized, each perspective is based on real things that happened to real people before and during the election. As you'll see, the same event can look different depending on one's point of view.

Chapter 1

Stephanie Harrison

Obama Volunteer

"Where are those envelopes?"

"I can't find the yard signs. Did someone move them?"

"I'm on the phone here, guys—be quiet!"

"Are we out of pizza?"

I stood in the middle of the room and listened to everyone yelling back and forth. The energy in our local **campaign** headquarters was amazing. Everyone was busy. Six people were at desks making phone calls. Three volunteers were on the computer, and five more workers were circling in search of office supplies or something to eat. I loved it here.

▲ *Campaign headquarters are places where people gather in their community to help a candidate get elected to a public office, like the presidency.*

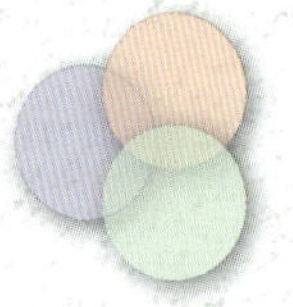

Think About It

- Read the paragraph about why the Harrison family supported Obama. What is the main point? Give two reasons why you think this.

My father was one of the senior volunteers for our city's Democratic Party. He helped organize everyone and made sure each job got done. This year, with Senator Barack Obama running, I had begged to join Dad at the center. I wanted to be involved. I thought the senator from Illinois was an amazing guy and would make a terrific president. I watched him on television during the **debates** and thought he did a great job. My mom liked his focus on hope and a "change we can believe in." My dad liked Obama's plans for reducing the troops in Iraq.

Dad sighed. "This place is a madhouse today," he said. He looked at me. "Ready to get started, Stephanie?"

I grinned. I was more than ready.

I began by refilling the coffee and then putting out the vegetable tray that Dad and I had brought from home.

▲ *Barack Obama served in the Illinois Senate, as well as the United States Senate, before running for president in the 2008 election.*

"Thanks, Steph," said Cindy, one of the volunteers. She grabbed a couple of pieces of celery. "I was getting pretty tired of cold pizza and stale doughnuts."

Next, I went over to the supply desk and started organizing it. I did this every time I came in—it was always a jumbled mess from people hurriedly grabbing what they needed. I stacked the door hangers that volunteers left at people's houses when they did their block walks. I put a new stack of envelopes on the table and placed markers and pens next to the notepads. Then I went into the back room and grabbed a pile of yard signs. I leaned them on the wall next to the supply desk where everyone could easily see them.

Second Source

- Finish reading this chapter, then find a second source that describes Sarah Palin's struggle in the media. Compare the information there to the information in this source.

▲ *Obama's wife, Michelle Obama, campaigned with her husband in 2008.*

▲ *Sarah Palin was mayor of Wasilla, Alaska, before becoming the state's first female governor in 2006.*

Finally, I got a roll of paper towels and a bottle of cleaner and started cleaning wherever I could. I wiped off the handles of the telephones that were not being used. These phones got a lot of use as volunteers called people throughout the city to encourage them to vote in the upcoming election. I also wiped off a few of the desks, gathered empty coffee cups, and swept around the food table.

"Good work, Steph," my dad said as he walked by.

Just then, a yell went up from a few of the volunteers. "Sarah Palin strikes again!" Debbie said.

I winced. John McCain's running mate for vice president had been ridiculed lately for her mistakes during important speeches and interviews. Now what had this Alaskan governor done?

"When Katie Couric (a CBS news anchor) asked Palin what specific resources she uses as news sources, the governor could not name a single one," Alex explained.

"She just said, 'Um, all of them, any of them that have been in front of me all these years,'" Michael added.

Oh dear, I thought. Not the best answer for a woman struggling to make a good impression on the American people.

"Back to work, people!" said my dad. "Let's focus on Obama's push for hope and change here."

▲ *The 2008 election saw the third-highest number of young voters (between the ages of 18 and 24) in a presidential election since 1972.*

"Comments like Palin's certainly make me hope for change," Elizabeth mumbled as she walked back to her desk.

"Where are those darn yard signs?" someone yelled. I chuckled. Clearly some things never change.

A New Outlet for News

During the 2008 election, the Internet played a bigger role than ever before. According to statistics, 74 percent of Internet users went online to get news and other information about the election. This was the first time that more than half of the voting-age population used the Internet to keep up with election details. The researchers reported that 60 percent went online for news, 38 percent to talk about politics with others, and 59 percent to e-mail, text, instant-message, post, or Tweet about the campaigns.

Chapter 2

Timothy Cooper

U.S. Army Soldier

"Beep, beep, beep!" The alarm clock chirped enthusiastically until I reached out to silence it.

Carefully, I sat up and shifted my right leg to better support me. I longingly thought of those mornings years ago when I could get out of bed easily and automatically, without having to first think about how to do it. Those days were gone. Ever since that rocket-propelled **grenade** had exploded a few feet away from me in Iraq, life had been very different. I sometimes dreamed about it at night. "Cooper! Hit the ground!" I could hear my sergeant screaming. He probably saved my life with that yell.

▲ *In 2003, the U.S. invaded Iraq. The president sent about 130,000 troops to the country.*

Now, whenever I wake up, for just a moment I feel like I can wiggle the toes on my left foot, even though the foot and calf were gone. It made me angry every time. I wished that, even though I had been **discharged** from the Army because of the injury, I could somehow go back and get revenge for what was done to me.

I flipped on the television to catch the news. As usual, it was about the election. I paused to watch for a moment since McCain was being interviewed. I respected the man for his years of service to this country. He was the son and grandson of Navy admirals and spent more than 20 years as a naval **aviator**. I remember hearing him talk about his time as a prisoner of war in 1967 when he had been captured by the North Vietnamese.

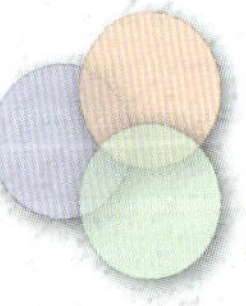

Second Source

- Find a second source that shows McCain's voting record on issues relating to soldiers and war veterans. How does that information compare to the information in this book?

"I fell in love with my country when I was a prisoner in someone else's," he had stated in a speech at the Republican National Convention last week. "I loved it because it was not just a place, but an idea, a cause worth fighting for. I was never the same again. I wasn't my own man anymore, I was my country's." I could relate to those feelings.

▲ *John McCain was a prisoner at the Hỏa Lò Prison in Hanoi, Vietnam. He spent over five years as a prisoner of war.*

Analyze This

- How is Timothy Cooper's perspective about what should be done in Iraq different from the Harrisons' perspective? How will his experiences affect whom he votes for?

Obama was a nice guy, but he was just too young and inexperienced to be president. He had never even served in any of the armed forces. He was a **liberal** who could not possibly relate to the worries and problems I had as an injured veteran. McCain could. He knew that we needed to send thousands more soldiers into Iraq, not cut back like Obama wanted to do. The Illinois senator had stated he would be the president who brought the troops home, but that was the wrong choice. As McCain said during a town hall meeting in New Hampshire, it was fine with him if the U.S. military remained in Iraq for a hundred years. He was right. We had to stay there until this war ended—no matter how long it took. No wonder McCain's **slogan** for this year's election was "Country First."

▲ *McCain has been in politics since 1982 when he was elected to the U.S. House of Representatives for Arizona.*

▲ *Both McCain and Obama supporters came out to Times Square in New York City to watch results come in on election day.*

I had yet another doctor's appointment today. I had lost count of how many I'd had so far. Getting quality health care had been quite a debated issue in this year's election. McCain had stated, "As president, I will do everything in my power to ensure that those who serve today and those who have served in the past have access to the highest quality health, mental health, and **rehabilitative** care in the world."

2008 Presidential Election Results

Candidate	Electoral College Vote	Popular Vote
Barack Obama	365	66.8 million
John McCain	173	58.3 million

I hoped he was right. Life was tough right now, and I needed a break. I just hoped that the future President McCain would be that extra boost I needed to cope with my life after Iraq.

Chapter 3

Leticia Tomlinson

Ohio Student

"Look at that! He just took California! That's another 55 votes," shouted my aunt Jillian. "Mama, look," she said to my grandmother Helen. "Senator Obama just won another state. He almost has enough **electoral college** votes to win."

"Did you see that, Leticia?" my mom asked me. She looked like someone had given her a gift, she was so happy. "This is a very important day for all African-Americans."

"Letty, darling, come here," my grandmother said, patting the open spot on the couch next to her. I hesitated. I was on my way to the kitchen to get a bowl of Grandma's famous peach cobbler. I could

▲ *Obama was the first African-American to be nominated for president by the Democratic or Republican party.*

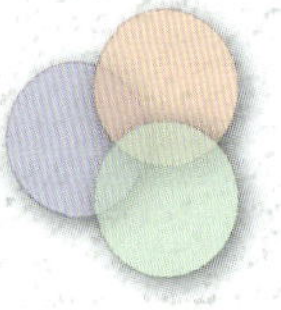

Analyze This

- How does being African-American impact how the Tomlinsons felt about Obama's election?

see she really wanted to talk to me, though, so I curled up next to her.

"I know you might take Mr. Obama's election for granted, but for the rest of us, this is nothing short of a miracle," Grandma explained. "I grew up on stories about my great-great-grandma, who was a slave. She was not allowed to go to school, get married, or even leave the plantation where she lived."

I did the math in my head and quickly realized that just seven generations ago, my family had been slaves. It was a life I couldn't even imagine.

"And you know, believe it or not, I remember when they finally ended **segregation** in the schools. I was only six years old at the time, but I heard my parents talking about it. I was excited to get the

▲ *Segregation in schools was ended in 1954 when the* Brown v. Board of Education *case determined that "separate but equal" schools under segregation were unconstitutional.*

chance to go to the white school," Grandma said with a chuckle. "I remember sitting in the back of buses, using separate drinking fountains, and not being allowed in certain places. I've never understood how the color of a person's skin had anything to do with his worth as a human being." She sat silently for a moment, lost in thoughts and memories.

"Then came the civil rights movement of the 1950s and 1960s, and the efforts to defend those rights gained through the 1970s," my mother said. "I was born in the early 1970s, but I listened to all the stories about Martin Luther King Jr. and the civil rights marches. I certainly have dealt with prejudice myself, despite all of our country's changes," she added sadly.

"It's too bad Rosa Parks did not live to see this day," Aunt Jillian said. "She would have been so thrilled to see a black man in the White House."

"Do you see why we are so happy about Barack Obama becoming our 44th president, Letty?" Grandma asked.

"We are hoping that his election will help the country learn to accept **diversity** and unity," Mom said.

"He ran with an emphasis on hope and change," Grandma said.

▲ *Obama won the 2008 presidential election with 53 percent of the popular vote. In 2012, he won a second term with 51 percent.*

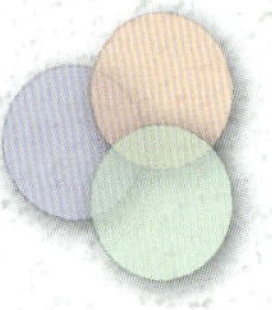

Second Source

- Find a second source that explains who Rosa Parks was. How does that information help you better understand what Aunt Jillian said?

"Let's hope that change is what he brings to all of us."

"Sssssh!" said Aunt Jillian. "They just announced that Obama has won."

We all turned to the television. "If there is anyone out there who still doubts that America is a place where all things are possible, who still wonders if the dream of our founders is alive in our time, who still questions the power of our democracy, tonight is your answer," the president-elect stated. "It's been a long time coming, but tonight, because of what we did on this date in this election at this defining moment, change has come to America."

As I looked across the room, I realized that more than three generations of experiences were present. The spirits of our ancestors were present, too, and they were cheering. For all African-Americans, it was time to celebrate—and a perfect time for peach cobbler!

Coming Together

In Obama's acceptance speech in 2008, he honored John McCain by stating, "Senator McCain fought long and hard in this campaign. And he's fought even longer and harder for the country that he loves. He has endured sacrifices for America that most of us cannot begin to imagine. We are better off for the service rendered by this brave and selfless leader." He spoke of looking forward to working with McCain after the election.

Look, Look Again

This photo shows a popular campaign poster for candidate Barack Obama. Use the photo to help you answer the questions below:

1. How would a worker for Obama's campaign feel seeing this photo? What about someone who worked for McCain's campaign?

2. What might a veteran who had fought for the United States think about this photo? Why?

3. Given the history of Obama's run for president, how might an African-American family feel about this photo?

Glossary

aviator (AY-vee-ay-tur) a pilot on an airplane or other type of aircraft

campaign (kam-PAYN) the competition by rival political candidates for public office

debates (dih-BAYTS) discussions in which people express different opinions

discharged (DIS-chahrjd) to be relieved or removed from a position

diversity (dih-VUR-sih-tee) variety or being different

electoral college (ih-LEK-tor-uhl KAH-lij) body of electors chosen by the voters in each state to elect the president and vice president of the United States

grenade (gruh-NADE) a small shell containing an explosive

liberal (LIB-ur-uhl) in favor of political progress and individual freedom

rehabilitative (ree-ha-BIH-lih-tay-tiv) an action that restores a person to good condition

segregation (seg-rih-GAY-shuhn) setting apart people from others, sometimes based on race

slogan (SLOH-guhn) a distinctive phrase for a party, group, or person

Learn More

Further Reading

Biskup, Agnieszka. *Obama: The Historic Election of America's 44th President.* Mankato, MN: Capstone Press, 2012.

Edwards, Roberta. *Barack Obama: United States President.* New York: Grosset & Dunlap, 2009.

Goodman, Susan. *See How They Run: Campaign Dreams, Election Schemes, and the Race to the White House.* New York: Bloomsbury, 2008.

Gorman, Jacqueline L. *Why Are Elections Important?* Pleasantville, NY: Weekly Reader Books, 2008.

Robinson, Tom. *John McCain: POW & Statesman.* Minneapolis: ABDO Publishing, 2010.

Williams, Spencer. *John McCain: An American Life.* New York: Grosset & Dunlap, 2008.

Web Sites

Congress for Kids—The Election of the President
www.congressforkids.net/Elections_electionpres.htm

Kids.gov—How to Become President of the USA Poster
https://kids.usa.gov/president/index.shtml

Index

About the Author

Tamra Orr remembers voting in the 2008 election and how exciting it was. She is the author of hundreds of books for readers of all ages. She lives in the Pacific Northwest with her family and spends all of her free time writing letters, reading books, and going camping. She graduated from Ball State University with a degree in English and education and believes she has the best job in the world. It gives her the chance to keep learning all about the world and the people in it.